BIONICLE™

CHRONICLES #1

Tale of the Toa

by C.A. Hapka

SCHOLASTIC INC.
New York Toronto London Auckland Sydney
Mexico City New Delhi Hong Kong Buenos Aires

ISBN 0-439-50116-4

Design by Peter Koblish

12 11 10 9 8 7 6 5   4 5 6 7 8/0

Printed in the U.S.A.
First printing, August 2003

The Legend of Mata Nui

In the time before time, the Great Spirit descended from the heavens, carrying we, the ones called the Matoran, to this island paradise. We were separate and without purpose, so the Great Spirit blessed us with three virtues: unity, duty, and destiny. We embraced these gifts and, in gratitude, we named our island home Mata Nui, after the Great Spirit himself.

But our happiness was not to last. Mata Nui's brother, Makuta, was jealous of these honors and betrayed him. Makuta cast a spell over Mata Nui, who fell into a deep slumber. Makuta's power dominated the land, as fields withered away, sunlight grew cold, and ancient values were forgotten.

Still, all hope was not lost. Legends told of six mighty heroes, the Toa, who would arrive to save Mata Nui. Time would reveal that these were not simply myths — for the Toa did appear on the shores of the island. They arrived with no memory, no knowledge of one another — but they pledged to defend Mata Nui and its people against the darkness. Tahu, Toa of Fire. Onua, Toa of Earth. Gali, Toa of Water. Lewa, Toa of Air. Pohatu, Toa of Stone. And Kopaka, Toa of Ice. Great warriors with great power, drawn from the very elements themselves. Together, they were six heroes with one destiny: to defeat Makuta and save Mata Nui.

This is their story.

TAHU — TOA OF FIRE

A beach. He was standing on a sweeping expanse of sand sloping gently down to the sea.

As he gazed out at the ocean, he saw waves breaking over a coral reef. Beyond that, there was nothing but water stretching to an unbroken horizon.

Where am I? he thought, his mind a haze of memories and dreams. *WHO am I?*

. . . Tahu . . .

The word — a name? — floated through his mind. It seemed to fit, to make sense somehow. But little else did.

Tahu shook his head in frustration. Why couldn't he remember more? How had he come to this place — and why?

He glanced toward the polished canister

that had brought him here. Near it he saw several red components lying on the sand. Two turned out to be blades, shaped into the form of leaping red flames. They fitted together into a sword, the handle sitting comfortably in his clawed hand. But when he swung the sword, it felt heavy and awkward.

He scowled. "Useless hunk of metal," he muttered, jabbing the blade into the sand.

Then he noticed the mask. It stared up at him with gaping eyeholes, its surface catching the sunlight so that it appeared to come alive in his hands. Taking a deep breath, Tahu lifted the mask to his face.

A surge of power coursed through him. Yes! This was more like it!

Tahu grabbed the flame sword and lifted it. This time, to his surprise, the blade was glowing with crimson fire. When he swung the sword, it sizzled through the air, trailing sparks in its wake.

"Yes!" Tahu said with grim satisfaction. "Now we're getting somewhere."

But was he? He let the sword fall to his

side, overwhelmed by despair. Why was he here? What was he supposed to do now?

"Why — can't — I — REMEMBER?" He howled, swinging his sword over his head.

A bolt of fiery energy shot forth, erupting into the sky like a volcano. Sparks showered down onto the beach, but Tahu didn't feel their heat.

Power . . . I have such power, he thought with wonder. *The power of fire. Of heat and flame. But where does it come from? What is it for?*

More questions — and still he had no answers. Not knowing made him shake with frustration and rage. It made him want to turn his sword against the earth, the sky, the beach — the very world itself. It was tempting — so tempting. To lose himself in chaos, to strike out with no thought for past, future, or anything else.

Tahu took a deep breath. No. He couldn't allow himself to give in. Somehow he knew that, just as he'd known his name.

Okay, okay, he told himself. *The knowing will come. At least . . . I hope it will.*

LEWA — TOA OF AIR

"This sturdy clingtwiner will do, I expect," the bright green figure murmured to himself, stretching to grab a thick vine that was hanging down in front of him. He glanced into the canyon below, then shook his head and grinned. "No secondthink, just go . . . !"

With that, he leaped off the tree branch overhanging the canyon. He swung himself halfway across, then let go. Momentum carried him in a graceful arc over and past the gorge.

He laughed with delight as he landed cleanly on a nearby tree.

"Now *that* was fun," he exclaimed.

He hadn't been sure that he could make such a leap. But now he knew at least one thing: The air was his friend!

He didn't know much else. He knew his name was Lewa. At least he thought so. He liked the name — it sounded strong and mysterious.

Lewa, mysteryking of know-nothingness, he thought with a smile. *That's me!*

He glanced down at himself, at his strong limbs the color of the jungle leaves. In one hand he carried an axlike blade, perfect for slicing through thick underbrush or twining foliage. Though he couldn't see it, he knew that his bright green mask swept back in a streamlined shape perfect for cutting through the air.

His smile faded as his mind flashed back to the dreams. Was that all they were? Dreams? He hoped so — for they had been dark and chaotic, and filled him with fear.

"Never mind," he muttered. "Time enough for darkthought later. It's time for some answer-finding."

Lewa had immediately found himself drawn to the lush, dripping jungle. Now that he was here, he felt at home.

As he reached the edge of a large stand of

Volo trees, Lewa jumped onto a slender branch. The motion flung something out of a nest of feathers and twigs farther along the branch.

He cried out in dismay, realizing that he had just ejected a baby Taku out of its nest. Without thought, he flung one arm upward through the air in the direction of the falling chick.

"Up you go!" he cried.

For a moment he thought that the baby bird was flying away. Then he realized the truth.

No, not flying — the wind had caught it and carried it aloft.

Leaping across to a closer branch, Lewa reached up and caught the chick gently in one hand. He placed it carefully back in its nest.

"Now, what kind of happyluck was that?" he murmured. "Or — or *was* it?"

Struck with a sudden impulse, he flung up his arm. Once again, a quick gust swooped up from below with a swirl of leaves.

"It was *me*!" Lewa breathed in amazement. "*I* did it. The wind answers to *me*!"

ONUA — TOA OF EARTH

Dig, pull, scrape, push. Dig, pull, scrape, push.

Onua fell into comfortable rhythm as he scooped out a new tunnel. He was happy to be underground.

But he still felt uneasy. Aside from his name, he didn't know anything about who or where he was. And he couldn't shake the feeling that he was somehow missing something — missing a piece of himself.

But he pushed that worry aside. There was no sense in wasting energy fretting over what he couldn't control. All he could do was control what he could — like the digging.

Onua powered his huge hand forward through a rocky section of the tunnel wall. It met empty air instead of earth and rock. Interesting.

Pushing through with a shower of stones and clay, Onua found himself in a large cavern. In the center, a tower of rock ended in a flat stone platform. Atop it, a lightstone glowed.

So there are others underground, Onua thought. *Perhaps they will have some answers for me.*

He spotted a tunnel in the far wall of the cavern and followed it.

Turning a corner, he was startled to see a familiar-looking figure at the center of a large mural.

"Is that — me?" he whispered, reaching out to touch the image. It portrayed a powerful-looking figure with a wedge-shaped mask and large clawed hands. The figure was standing among five other, similar figures.

As Onua touched the lines of the carving, he felt a strange vibration in the wall. Stepping forward, he put his head to it, listening intently.

Thunka thunka thunka thunka thunka . . .

It was a steady rhythm. Onua had no idea what it meant. But he planned to find out.

With one last glance at the picture of himself, he turned and continued down the tunnel, keeping one hand on the wall to follow the vibrations.

The pulsing grew stronger and stronger — and with the next twist of the tunnel, Onua found what he was looking for. Another enormous cavern lay before him, lit by more lightstone platforms. Dozens of stone columns stretched up to the high ceiling. Between these columns were paths made of cobblestones set into the earthen floor. Stone benches stood beside the paths, and a small, clear stream trickled through the cavern.

It must be a — a park of some sort, Onua realized. *But — down here? Why — and how?*

Stepping forward, he saw that the little stream emptied out into a still, round pool lined with pebbles. In the center, reddish-brown gemstones spelled out a word:

ONU-KORO

Onu-Koro — what did that mean? What kind of connection did it have with his name?

Before he had time to ponder this, Onua saw a small figure hurrying across the park.

Onua leaped forward. "You there!" he called. "Hey, hello!"

The figure glanced over his shoulder, then stopped short. "Oh!" he exclaimed. "Oh, oh."

Onua frowned. Perhaps this being didn't speak the same language as he did. He cleared his throat. "Hel-lo," he said as slowly and clearly as he could. "Me — Onua." He put a hand to his chest, then pointed toward the other. "Who — you? Do — you — understand — me?"

"Oh, yes!" the small figure cried, bending into a sort of hurried bow. "Oh, Toa Onua — we have been waiting for you such a long time! Come, please — Turaga Whenua will want to see you right away."

Confused, Onua followed him. "You know my name," he said. "But I don't know yours."

"Oh! Forgive my rudeness, Toa. My name is Onepu. I am a Matoran of this village of Onu-Koro."

Onepu led the way through a series of tunnels and caverns. Soon they reached another large cavern. On each wall, a series of carved-out dwellings climbed nearly to the ceiling.

"Wait here, please, Toa," Onepu said, gesturing toward a large stone bench near the fountain. "I will fetch the Turaga."

Onua nodded, and the Matoran rushed off. Onua took the opportunity to look around. At the center of the cavern was a fountain filled with crystal-clear water. A sculpture arose from the pool, spouting water out of several spots.

Onua blinked. Was he going crazy, or did that sculpture look an awful lot like — him?

He was still staring at the fountain when he heard someone behind him. Turning, he saw a figure much like Onepu, but a bit taller and with a different mask. The eyes behind that mask held patience, caution, and great wisdom.

"I am Whenua, Turaga of this village," the stranger said, bowing. "Welcome, Toa Onua. We have been awaiting you."

"Yes, so I've heard," Onua replied. "And I've been awaiting some clue about who I am and what I'm doing here."

"The legends said that would be the case," Whenua said. "It was said that the Toa, when they arrived, would remember very little."

"You said when 'they' arrived," Onua said. "Are there — are there others like me?"

Whenua nodded. "There are five others," he said. "Each of you draws his power from a different element — yours is the earth itself. Your purpose is to use that power to face and fight a mighty evil — Makuta."

Though Onua wasn't sure why, the name sent a chill through him. An image floated into his mind — dark, empty eyes in an even darker face shrouded with gray smoke.

"Makuta?" Onua repeated as the image floated away. "Who or what is this Makuta?"

"He is the darkness, the essence of chaos and emptiness and fear, the spirit of destruction," Whenua replied in a trembling voice. "It is said that only the Toa have the power to stand against him."

"'It is said'?" Onua asked. "You don't sound too certain about our success."

Whenua shook his head sadly. "It serves no purpose to be false, for the earth cannot be deceived," he said. "Nothing about your quest is certain, except that it is your duty to try. That is all that any of us can do in this life."

"I will do what I can," he promised solemnly. "But first, you must tell me all you know of these powers you say I have."

"Of course, Toa," Whenua said. "For that is *my* duty. First, you should know that the power itself comes from within you, but it is focused through your mask — the Pakari, the Great Mask of Strength."

"My — my mask?" Onua touched his hand to his face, remembering the surge of strength and power when he'd first put it on.

Whenua nodded somberly. "The Pakari gives you power — great power," he said. "But one mask will not be enough. . . ."

GALI — TOA OF WATER

The waters lifted her, carrying her along in a soft current of warmth. She didn't know who or where she was, but she knew she belonged here in the calm, cool blue of the sea. That was perhaps the only thing she knew for sure.

That and her name: Gali.

But I can't just float here forever, she reminded herself. *I have things to do. If only I knew what they were . . .*

She had no certain memories, but many uncertain ones — fragments of thoughts and images. There was urgency in those fragments, though some of them hinted at peace as well. Especially one, an endless sea of calm waters surrounding an island, embracing it and soothing its ills . . .

Gali kicked swiftly forward with her flipperlike feet. Her hooked arms cut through the water, and the ridged edges on her blue mask sent bubbly ripples out to the sides as she swam. The sea was full of life, but Gali felt strangely alone.

As she swam, she felt a shivering tremor radiate through the water. A brightly colored eel raced past her. Several schools of fish followed.

Gali paused and stared in the direction the creatures had come. What had frightened them?

More fish rushed past her in a panic, along with several crabs and snails and even a small shark. Gali pushed forward, swimming against the tide of fleeing sea creatures.

A large coral reef blocked her view of whatever lay beyond. As she swam around it, Gali saw a gigantic creature barreling toward her. The water churned around its vicious-looking snout as its long, powerful arms pulled it forward toward Gali faster and faster.

Gali gasped. She had no idea what the monster might be, but she could see why the other creatures had fled. The predator wore a dingy-looking, ugly mask over its triangular face, and its gleaming red eyes were ruthless and savage.

There was no time to outswim the huge creature — it was already too close. For a fraction of a second Gali thought of using the coral reef for protection. But she couldn't stand to imagine the creature crashing through the delicate structures, destroying the living coral.

Gali let her instincts take over. Pushing off of the coral, she bulleted through the water off to one side. Then she shot toward the surface. She broke the surface and extended her arms, not sure why she was doing so.

She felt the waters gather and respond to her call. As the giant sea creature burst to the surface a short distance away, an enormous wave formed around her. Her vicious pursuer leaped forward, but the tidal wave rocketed Gali away toward the shore, faster than any creature could swim. Gali smiled as the water carried her to safety. *So this is what I am meant to do,* she thought. *I am here to command the seas. But for what purpose?*

A few minutes later, Gali shook herself dry as she stepped out of the surf onto the beach. She stood there for a moment, looking around, strangely reluctant to leave the water.

She glanced across the beach. A thick, dripping jungle began where the sands left off. The humidity of the place reached out, beckoning to her, and she could not resist its call.

POHATU — TOA OF STONE

Pohatu glanced over his shoulder. On the wall that surrounded the village of Po-Koro, dozens of Matoran were gathered, watching him go. Grinning, Pohatu shaded his eyes with one hand and gave them a quick wave with the other. The villagers waved back and cheered.

"That was an interesting visit," Pohatu said aloud to himself as he turned away again. "It's not every day you find out you're the Toa of Stone."

He almost tripped on a protruding stone in the path. Glancing down, he saw three words spelled out in cobblestones beneath his feet —

UNITY

DUTY

DESTINY

"Hmm, now where have I heard those words before?" Pohatu murmured with a chuckle. The Turaga of Po-Koro had told him of many things — the strange, dark history of this island of Mata Nui, the mysterious masks that were hidden throughout the island, and best of all that there were five other Toa with powers as strong as his own.

As the village elder spoke, three words had come up again and again — unity, duty, destiny. These three concepts had given the Matoran a purpose, something to strive for always.

Now it was time to see the rest of this island. *Turaga Onewa said this mask I wear is the Kanohi Kakama, the Great Mask of Speed,* Pohatu thought. *Maybe it's time to put it to the test.*

He hesitated, wondering if it was wise to experiment with his powers when he still knew so little about how they worked.

But what was the worst that could happen? Gathering his energy, Pohatu directed his gaze toward the top of Mount Ihu — and ran.

The desert landscape passed in a yellowish blur, all details obscured by the Toa's immense speed. After a moment the yellowish blur shifted into a brown one punctuated by flashes of green, and then quickly grew paler again until all Pohatu could see around him was white.

He slowed to a stop. He was standing in a snowdrift overlooking a frozen lake. The steep, icy slopes of Mount Ihu rose above him.

"Outrageous," he said breathlessly, a smile spreading behind his mask. "Now *that's* what I call speed!"

Leaving the frozen lake behind, he started up the mountainside. The Turaga had told him the main temple, the Kini-Nui, was in the exact center of the island on the far side of Mount Ihu. It seemed as likely a place as any to look for the other Toa.

As he turned around to check his progress, he caught a glimpse of movement somewhere farther up the slopes. A bird?

"Not unless this island grows its birds awfully big," he muttered, staring at the silver-and-white figure gliding gracefully down a high mountain slope, powdery snow flying up in an arc behind his feet. No, there was only one thing it could be. Another Toa!

His heart pounding, Pohatu leaped up the slopes, gathering speed — careful not to go *too* fast. He didn't want to overshoot his target.

He lost sight of his quarry for a few minutes as he tromped through a narrow valley. Grumbling at the snowdrifts, which came up to his waist in some spots, he glanced upward. At the top of the valley, a rocky bluff hid the higher slopes from his view. He clambered up toward it, finally leaving the deeper snowdrifts behind. Brushing the snow from his body, Pohatu gazed at the precipice standing in his way. If he had judged the distance right, the other Toa should be on the snowy slope just on the other side.

"Time for a shortcut," Pohatu murmured. "I don't want him to start skiing down that hill and get away from me. Besides, I might as well start getting used to this power of mine. . . ."

Taking a deep breath, he hunched his shoulders and raced straight at the solid stone.

KOPAKA — TOA OF ICE

Rumble . . . rumble . . . CRAAAAAAASSSH!

Kopaka's ice blade was up and ready as the rocky bluff exploded. But there was no time to dodge as enormous boulders rained down around him.

"Watch out!" a voice cried from somewhere in the storm of stone.

Kopaka lifted his shield, protecting himself as best he could. When the eruption of stone stopped, he found himself trapped between several huge boulders.

Glancing up, he saw a figure about his own size gazing down at him, resting his weight on one of the large stones. The stranger wore a bronze-colored mask, and the eyes behind it were concerned and a bit sheepish.

"Sorry about that," the stranger said. "I was practicing. Are you all right?"

"I would be," Kopaka returned icily. "If you weren't standing on me."

The stranger jumped back a few steps, then stretched out his arm. "Let me help you out."

Kopaka was already pointing his ice blade at the nearest rock. He was annoyed that the stranger's sudden appearance had taken him by surprise, caught him with his defenses down. He would not make that mistake again.

"Thank you. I don't need help," he said.

Focusing his energy, he channeled it through the blade. A thrill ran through him as the rock around him froze solid, becoming brittle and glassy.

The other figure was still watching him anxiously. "Let me do it," he urged as Kopaka lifted his blade again. "It'll be faster."

Kopaka frowned, already tired of the stranger's pushy chatter. "I said, I can do it myself!" Bringing the blade down, he smashed the icy boulder into smithereens, freeing himself.

The stranger looked impressed for a moment. Then he shrugged. "Yeah, well, you missed one," he said, kicking at one remaining boulder.

Kopaka blinked as the huge stone went sailing off toward the horizon. Whoever this stranger was, he was strong — incredibly strong. Kopaka supposed that meant he had to be one of the other Toa that Turaga Nuju had mentioned.

But Kopaka had no interest in meeting other Toa.

Turning away from the stranger, he continued on his way. The Matoran had told him there was a mask at the top of this mountain — the Place of Far-seeing, they had called it. He meant to find that mask as soon as possible.

But the stranger didn't get the message. "Hey," he called. "Wait! Are you a Toa? I've been looking for you — I am Pohatu, Toa of Stone."

Kopaka considered not answering — maybe if he ignored this annoying Pohatu, he would go away. But it seemed unlikely.

"Kopaka," he said brusquely. "Ice. And if you don't mind, I'm in the middle of something. See you later." He bent and effortlessly rode a slight dip in the ground, his feet sliding smoothly over the ice. He soon left Pohatu behind.

But it turned out that the newcomer was not to be abandoned so easily. "Wait!" he called again, scrabbling up the hill. "Listen, I have a feeling we're both here for the same reason. Why not team up? It might make things easier."

"I work alone."

"By choice?" Pohatu returned quickly. "Or just because no one can stand you?"

Kopaka almost smiled at that. Almost. This other Toa was irritating and far too chatty, but he also seemed to be quick-witted. And he was certainly strong. Perhaps he could come in handy after all. Especially if they came across another of those huge, vicious creatures that the Matoran called Rahi . . .

"All right," Kopaka said after a long moment. "Come along. After all, I might need a mountain moved — or the island lifted."

Pohatu chuckled. "Okay," he said. "So — where are we going, anyway? Should we start looking for masks, or seek the other Toa first?"

Kopaka pointed toward the peak rising just above them. Then he climbed on, not bothering to check whether Pohatu was following.

A few minutes later the two of them were standing at the peak of the mountain. Kopaka immediately spotted a mask lying in the snow.

Pohatu saw it, too. "Good work, brother," he said. "Go ahead — claim your prize."

Kopaka nodded. The new Kanohi looked gray and lifeless lying in the snow. Though it was the same size as his own mask, its shape was different — a helmetlike form with angled eyes and three slashes in each cheek.

The Kanohi Hau, Kopaka thought, remembering what the Turaga had told him. *The Great Mask of Shielding*.

Kopaka bent to pick up the mask. He stared at it for a moment, then carefully placed it over his own mask. Immediately, a strange feeling overwhelmed him. As if a cushion of strength had settled in around him, protecting him from all harm.

But what of his other powers? Did this new mask affect them? Kopaka called forth the power of his original mask, which gave him the ability to see through stone and snow to what lay beneath. Glancing down at the ground, he saw the icy snow . . . and then the raw, cold dirt underneath . . . and below that, a layer of rock crosscut with veins of minerals.

"The powers of the Mask of Vision are still mine to use." He was pleased.

As he turned his gaze toward the south, his X-ray vision cut straight through the craggy bluffs to several bright spots of color far below in the foothills. Then he sighed. For a moment he was tempted to turn away, to ignore what he'd seen. But he realized he might as well face up to the inevitable.

"We have to go," he told Pohatu abruptly, hating the thought of what was to come but knowing there was no avoiding it. "Now."

"Why?"

"No questions." Kopaka was tired of all the conversation. "Just follow me."

The two of them headed down the mountain, Pohatu skidding and slipping on the icy slopes. Kopaka forced himself to move slowly so the other Toa could keep up.

They were about halfway down when there was an earth-shattering roar from somewhere just ahead of them.

"Uh-oh," Pohatu said. "I don't like the sound of *that*."

Before Kopaka could respond, a massive creature burst through a snowbank a short distance below where the Toa were standing, sending a shower of snow and ice shards out on all sides. Kopaka shielded his eyes, squinting at the enormous, snorting, puffing beast as it skidded to a stop just a few lengths away.

"Is *this* what you were leading us toward?" Pohatu shouted, sounding dismayed.

"No," Kopaka said grimly.

The creature was like something out of a nightmare. Its red eyes gleamed with hate, and it pawed at the snowy ground with hooflike feet, puffs of steam blowing from its nostrils. Twin horns twisted out of the sides of its enormous head.

"Hmm," Pohatu said. "Do you think this big fellow is an ally or enemy?"

Kopaka glanced at him, startled, then realized the other Toa was kidding. He rolled his eyes, not amused. "Come on," he said. "I think we'd better —"

At that moment the hideous creature let out another thunderous bellow — and then charged straight at them.

"— run!" Pohatu finished for him.

The two Toa turned and sprinted back up the slope. At least Kopaka sprinted. Pohatu tried to run, but lost his footing on the ice and went down, struggling to keep himself from sliding right back under the beast's charging hooves.

Kopaka skidded to a stop, realizing the other Toa was in trouble. Big, charging, snorting trouble. Letting out a sigh, he skied back down the hill.

"No! Kopaka, don't — it's too dangerous."

"Don't be ridiculous." Kopaka waved his arms and shouted, trying to distract the enemy.

The creature slowed, glancing from one

Toa to the other, confused. Then it snorted and bellowed and returned its full attention to the fallen Pohatu, who was just now climbing unsteadily to his feet.

Time for Plan B, Kopaka thought, looking around for new ideas. They were standing on an open field that offered little in the way of hiding places. To one side, the ground dropped away sharply into a deep, icy ravine. Kopaka paused, his mind clicking into gear. If only he could get the beast to change directions . . .

There was just one problem — the creature was almost on top of Pohatu. Two more leaps, and its horns would be buried in the other Toa's chest. There would be no time to explain.

He'll just have to go with it, Kopaka told himself grimly, already pushing off smoothly and gathering speed as he skied downhill toward the fallen Toa. *If he doesn't, well . . .*

There was no sense worrying.

"Here goes nothing," he muttered.

SNORT! The beast made another leap forward. It lowered its head, aiming its horns directly at Pohatu. Pohatu took a step backward, almost falling again as his foot hit an icy patch.

Meanwhile, Kopaka skied toward him, gathering speed. This would be close. . . .

"Heads up!" he shouted. "And arms OUT!"

Pohatu looked startled, but flung his arms out to his sides.

Just as the creature lunged forward, snorting eagerly, Kopaka whizzed past and grabbed Pohatu around the chest.

"OOOOF!" Pohatu grunted as Kopaka yanked him out of the beast's path just as it lunged forward and buried its horns in the snow.

Kopaka wobbled, nearly losing his balance.

I have to straighten out, he thought. *Otherwise we'll never make it.* Behind him, he could already hear the beast roaring with anger and charging after them.

"Where — are — we — going?" Pohatu panted. To Kopaka's relief, the Stone Toa was hanging loosely in his arms, not struggling against his grip or trying to free himself.

Kopaka couldn't have replied even if he'd

wanted to. He was too busy willing his feet to obey him, in a desperate attempt to control the angle of their speedy downhill slide.

It worked. Just three or four lengths from the ravine now, his feet finally settled smoothly into an upright position on the icy snow. He bent as low as he could without dragging Pohatu's legs in the snow. Now there was no turning back. . . .

"Hey!" Pohatu cried, suddenly looking forward and seeing the chasm directly in front of them. "What are you — *AAAAAAAAAAAAH!*"

Kopaka held his breath as he felt his feet leave the cold, solid surface of the ice. He held on tightly to Pohatu as they flew up — up — up and over the canyon.

Pohatu was still screaming, but Kopaka didn't let out his breath until he felt his feet slam down again on the far side of the gorge. He teetered and threw himself to the side, allowing himself and Pohatu to pitch face-first into the snow.

"What the — why did you do that?" Pohatu cried, spitting out a mouthful of snow. "You could have gotten us killed!"

"That's why." Kopaka had already turned to stare back at the ravine. He pointed, and Pohatu turned to look just in time to see the snorting, squealing creature skid down the ice and tumble head over hooves into the depths of the fissure. A furious bellow drifted up toward them.

"Oh." Pohatu was silent for a moment. Then he grinned weakly. "Er, thanks. Guess I owe you one — brother."

Kopaka nodded. Then he crawled forward to the edge of the ravine, glancing down. The beast was still bellowing and struggling at the bottom, digging its hooves into the ice as it started to climb.

"It will be able to climb out of there soon enough," Kopaka observed, watching as the beast leaped up to an icy ledge.

"Not if I have anything to say about it," Pohatu replied. He climbed to his feet and strode toward the rocky cliff nearby. "You might want to step aside," he called over his shoulder as he began climbing hand over hand up the sheer rock face.

Kopaka moved a little farther down the slope, keeping an eye on the edge of the gulch. That beast could come charging out of there at any moment. . . .

"YEEEEE-HAW!" Pohatu cried, drawing his foot back and then kicking at a huge chunk of the rock face. The solid stone cracked instantly, and an enormous boulder flew forward, toward the fissure, disappearing over its edge.

Pohatu moved on to another section of the bluff. Once again he aimed a mighty kick, sending a chunk of stone across the snowy ground and straight into the gorge. Kopaka watched with grudging admiration as Pohatu repeated the movement again and again.

"Okay, this is too slow," Pohatu exclaimed. "Let's try something else."

What was he up to now? Kopaka had no idea. A second later Pohatu brought both fists down on the rock — and the cliff exploded into a thousand shards of stone.

Remembering his first meeting with Pohatu, Kopaka covered his head with his shield. A few pebbles bounced off of it, but the bulk of the explosion of stone showered down into the ravine with a deafening roar.

"Whoa!" Pohatu shouted gleefully after the noise had subsided. "That was so cool! I mean, I was pretty sure it would work, but still . . ."

While he waited for the other Toa to re-join him, Kopaka stepped forward and peered again over the edge of the chasm. The creature was buried up to its horns in the rocky mess that now filled nearly half of the deep canyon.

Hearing Pohatu hurrying up beside him, Kopaka turned. "Nice work," he said. "It will be able to escape — but not for a long while."

Pohatu glanced once more at the huge beast trapped below them. "That was close, though. What *is* that thing, anyway?"

"Rahi," Kopaka told him, already turning to lead the way down the snowy slope. "That's what the Turaga said they're called. There are many species, all shapes and sizes. They're not very friendly."

"No kidding."

Both Toa were silent for a few minutes as they climbed and skidded down the mountain, each buried in his own thoughts. Finally, Pohatu spoke again.

"So what did you see up there, anyway?" he asked. "From the peak, I mean."

This time, Kopaka decided to answer. "Strangers," he replied. "Beings of great power."

They came to the top of a steep hill. Standing in an open area below, four bright spots stood out against the drab background of stone and dirt. Four figures — one a bright, burning red, another blue as the sea, a third black as starless midnight, and the final one the same bright green as the leaves on the trees.

Kopaka stared down at them. The other Toa. It had to be them.

"But are they allies," he murmured, "or enemies?"

THE MEETING

Gali was the first to notice the two new-comers. "Brothers," she said quietly. "Look."

One of the newcomers wore a bronze mask. He leaped easily down to land among them. "Mind if we join the party?"

Tahu stepped forward. "I am Tahu, Toa of Fire. Who are you?"

The bronze stranger seemed unintimi-dated by Tahu's fiery glare. "I'm Pohatu," he said. "Toa of Stone. My talkative friend there is the Ice Toa, Kopaka." He gestured to the silver-and-white figure standing silently behind him.

The second newcomer stepped forward. Kopaka. Gali looked him up and down, feeling a chill ripple through the air as he came closer.

This one — this one has many layers, she

thought uncertainly. *He is cold. But I sense his frosty exterior may hide a blazing fire deep within. . . .*

At that moment, Kopaka turned his icy gaze upon her, catching her stare. He said nothing, but Gali quickly turned away.

More introductions were made, and soon they were trading stories of how and where they each had awakened.

As the others chatted, Kopaka said little. He was thinking about the future. What else lay in store for them here? And what of the mysterious Makuta, the evil one his villagers had spoken of?

He glanced at the red one, Tahu, who was blustering on about his journey to find his village, Ta-Koro, at the top of a volcano. *This Fire Toa is full of hot air*, Kopaka thought. *Will he be prepared for the heat of battle, or will he burn out quickly?*

Then there was Onua, the Toa of Earth. He spoke less than the others, while listening to all that was said. Did that subdued exterior hide a busy mind, or an empty one?

Just then Lewa, the Toa of Air, punctuated a comment he'd made by backflipping up onto a nearby boulder and doing a handstand. *So much energy,* Kopaka thought. *But it blows out of him uncontrolled, in all directions, like the wind. Not exactly someone I'd want to trust my life to in a tough spot.*

Hearing Pohatu's cheerful laugh, Kopaka turned to gaze at him. The Toa of Stone had surprised him in their battle against the horned Rahi. He had fought bravely. He had also been willing to entrust his life to Kopaka in that wild ski jump over the ravine.

I don't know if I could have done the same, Kopaka admitted to himself. Then he shook his head. *But why should he trust someone he doesn't know? It turned out well in that case, but he was foolish to be so ready to turn his life over to a stranger. I would not make that same mistake.*

Finally Kopaka turned his gaze toward Gali. Now this was one he couldn't read. The way he had caught her looking at him a few moments ago — it was as if she could see into his mind, his heart, just the way he could see through the earth and stone with his Mask of Vision. But that was impossible. Wasn't it?

Gali spoke, interrupting Kopaka's thoughts. "Well, brothers," she said, turning her gaze to take in all of them. "I suppose that's enough talk of the past. We should start discussing what comes next, yes? For despite all the interesting elemental powers we may have, I expect that our best weapon is our minds."

Kopaka almost smiled. At last, someone was talking sense!

"You're right, Gali," Tahu said. "We need to find these masks we seek — as quickly as possible. The Turaga of my village told me they will give us great powers. I know my own mask gives me the powers of protection or shielding. . . ."

"That's right," Pohatu interrupted. "Brother Kopaka has found a Mask of Shielding, too."

Tahu frowned. "Yes," he said shortly, sounding irritated. "Well, there are five more masks out there for each of us."

Once again, Kopaka held back a smile. Obviously Tahu was annoyed that someone else had beaten him to the first mask.

Onua looked thoughtful. "According to my

Turaga, the masks are hidden all over the island and Makuta has set his Rahi creatures to guard them. So our quest won't be easy."

"Fine, fine." Tahu sounded impatient. "Anyway, the important thing is to find them — fast. We'll split into smaller groups. Gali and Lewa, you can search the jungle and beaches together. Onua and Kopaka can check the caves of Onu-Wahi. And Pohatu, you can come with —"

"Hold on a quicksecond, brother Tahu," Lewa interrupted. "If speed is what we're after, why bother with the pairmaking? Why not each of us journeysearch on our own?"

Onua shrugged. "Our fiery brother has a good plan," he said calmly. "Working in pairs makes sense. It strikes a balance between speed and caution."

Gali was shaking her head. "Brothers, we have been brought together for a reason. I think we ought to stick together, at least until we know exactly what we're up against."

Pohatu nodded. "She's right," he said. "Trust me, these Rahi creatures are nothing to face alone. But if we travel together they should give us little trouble. Right, Kopaka?"

Kopaka shrugged, doing his best to chill the impatience he felt in listening to this conversation. Why hadn't he already departed? "I can't agree, Toa of Stone," he said. "We should split up. As I already told you, I prefer to work alone."

Pohatu looked slightly hurt. "You may prefer it," he replied. "But would you also prefer being chased by that sharp-horned beast if I hadn't been there to help you trap it?"

"Enough of this bickering," Tahu broke in impatiently. "We will accomplish nothing by standing here and having a debate. The decision is made — we split into small groups. It's the best of both worlds, can't you see that?"

All I see is one who believes that power belongs to whoever shouts the loudest, Kopaka thought in disgust. *Well, I, for one, am not ready to bow to such a 'leader.' Not as long as I have life in my body.*

Tahu noticed Kopaka's stare. What thoughts lay behind his mask? The Ice Toa's silence and intense gaze made Tahu uneasy, though he didn't like to admit it even to himself.

It doesn't matter, Tahu told himself, pushing such feelings aside. *There are more important things to worry about.*

The others were already back to arguing, several of them speaking at once.

CRRRRRRAAAAAAAAAK!

Suddenly, with no warning, the very earth yawned open in front of them, splitting the clearing in half. All around, the earth shuddered and trembled, smaller cracks opening here and there as the trees shook and birds took off into the air in a panic of cries.

Jagged streaks of white-hot lightning streaked across the sky, striking down only a few lengths from where the Toa stood.

"Get back!" Onua shouted as the air crackled with electricity and several trees and shrubs burst into flame.

Tahu leaped away with the others, though the fire held no terror for him. What was happening? A huge bank of dark clouds rolled in above them, releasing a torrent of rain and hail. A violent gust of wind howled down from farther up the mountain.

"What kind of crazystorm is this?" Lewa yelled over the noise of the pounding rain and shrieking wind. "An earthquake, thunder and lightning, rain and hail and wind all at once?"

Gali shook her head, shielding her face against the driving wind. "This can be no regular storm," she cried. "It must be the work of Makuta."

As the word left her mouth, the storm suddenly stopped. The earth lay still. The only hint of the storm was the smoldering remains of the lightning-scorched foliage — and the huge, gaping fissure in the ground.

"Eerie," Pohatu remarked.

Tahu nodded grimly. "Clearly, Makuta knows we're here. There is no time to lose. We need to find those masks — now."

WHAT LIES BENEATH

Tahu hadn't had a destination in mind when he had stomped off from the group of Toa. He was too angry to think straight.

No matter how often he had repeated his plan to split into pairs, the other Toa had refused to agree with it. Kopaka and Lewa had insisted on taking off on their own. Even Gali had seemed too distracted to argue the point — she was the only one among them who hadn't visited her village, and she was eager to find it now. And so the Toa had all gone their separate ways.

Tahu's anger drove him aimlessly over the foothills around the base of Mount Ihu, then onto the fiery slopes of the volcano.

Kopaka found one of his masks up there in the snow of his own homeland, Tahu thought as he headed up the fiery mountain. *Why shouldn't I start my search here in my own home region?*

Thinking about Kopaka made him clench his fist tighter on the handle of his fire sword.

It's like he just sits back and listens to us talk, thinking he's better than us, Tahu thought with a snort. *Like it's not worth his time to get involved.*

"It's not worth *my* time to worry about the likes of him," he said aloud. "Especially now . . ." He swung his sword to punctuate the point, accidentally sending a finger of flame shooting out and melting a nearby pile of stones into lava.

"With all due respect, great Toa, you might want to watch where you point that thing," a voice said from nearby.

Tahu whirled around. Standing before him was the broad-shouldered, sturdy-looking figure of a Ta-Matoran.

"I know you," the Toa said. "It's Jala, right?"

The Matoran nodded and bowed. "I am the Captain of the Guard of your village of Ta-Koro."

"Hello again," Tahu said. "And while

we're giving out advice, you might not want to sneak up on a Toa. It could be hazardous to your health."

"Sorry, Toa," Jala said with a grin. "I didn't mean to startle you."

"Apology accepted. But what was your intention in tracking me here?"

Jala's expression turned serious. "I came to see how your search for the masks was going. Don't take this the wrong way, but . . . do you have any kind of plan for finding them?"

Tahu frowned, feeling his fiery temper rising. How dare this lowly Matoran question his tactics?

"Of course I have a plan," he snapped. "I'm searching . . . I'm searching for the masks . . . Okay. Perhaps I don't have an exact plan as such. But I'm working on it."

Jala bowed again. "Of course, Toa," he said. "In any case, I thought it might be helpful for you to know that legend has it that a Kanohi Akaku — a Great Mask of X-Ray Vision — lies within the deepest cavern of Onu-Wahi."

"Onu-Wahi," Tahu repeated. "Those caves and tunnels that Onua spoke of?"

"Yes," Jala replied. "The network of underground passageways lies beneath much of Mata Nui. There is an entrance just over that way, beyond that lavastone wall. It leads to —"

"Thanks," Tahu interrupted, turning away.

"Toa Tahu!" Jala called after him. "Wait!"

Tahu paused, glancing over his shoulder. "Yes? What is it?" he demanded impatiently.

Jala touched one fist to his mask in a salute. "I just wanted to wish you luck," he said. "Take care in the dark underground. We just got you — we don't want to lose you again."

Tahu smiled. "Worry not," he said. "You'll not get rid of me so easily."

With that, he leaped over the wall and hurried toward the cave opening that lay beyond.

It wasn't long before Tahu realized why the Matoran had been so worried. Everything about the dark, twisting tunnels of Onu-Wahi felt wrong.

Even with the glow cast by his fire sword, the darkness seemed to huddle around him, suffocating in its closeness.

Taking a deep breath, he forced himself to move on. Some dark part of his mind protested — *No! We don't belong here, we shouldn't be here, we'll be crushed. . . .*

But Tahu shook his head fiercely, willing such thoughts away.

The air grew cold and still. The flame on his sword sputtered and flickered, but the force of his will kept it burning.

Almost there, he told himself grimly. *I can feel it. These tunnels can't possibly go much deeper.*

And yet they did. Deeper, and deeper, and deeper, until Tahu started to wonder if he hadn't just imagined that there was a surface world at all. Deeper — until he started seeing strange shapes moving in the shadows just beyond his glowing red light. And still deeper.

Finally he stepped out of the end of a tunnel into an enormous cavern. A raw, howling wind whipped through it. Only steps ahead, the floor dropped away into nothingness. Tahu couldn't see the bottom.

Great. Just great, he thought bitterly. *What am I supposed to do now?*

He wasn't sure what made him look up then, but as he did, he caught the glint of something across the chasm. Squinting against the darkness beyond his sword glow, he made out the vague shape of a ledge on the opposite wall of the cavern. On that ledge was a small gray shape — a mask? He wasn't sure.

In any case, the yawning depths of the chasm lay between him and the object. How was he supposed to get over there?

Tahu took a few careful steps along the near wall of the cavern. As he neared the edge, he finally spotted the answer to his problem — a bridge. A narrow stone span, stretching out from the wall and disappearing into the darkness.

The damp wind chilled him as he stood for a moment, uncertain. Then he shook his head. He hadn't come this far to turn back now.

He stepped out onto the bridge. It was even narrower than it had looked, and it took all of Tahu's concentration to maintain his balance.

After a few minutes he seemed no closer to the far ledge than when he'd started. *This is ridiculous*, he thought impatiently. *It's going to take forever to get across at this rate.*

He swung his foot out, taking a larger step this time. When it touched the rock, it skidded slightly to one side just as another violent wind gust swept past — and Tahu suddenly felt himself slipping sideways into the chasm!

He grabbed at the bridge, wrapping his left arm around it and holding tight. His legs swung loose over the abyss. He threw his right hand up and over the bridge as well, nearly losing his grip on his sword as he did so. With a grunt, he flung his legs up, clinging upside down to the underside of the bridge.

He focused on pulling himself up and to one side, inching his way around to the top of the bridge. Finally he heaved a breath of relief as he pulled himself right side up once again. After resting for a moment, he pushed himself into a crouch, and then back into a standing position.

Okay, slow and steady it is, then, Tahu told himself. *One foot in front of the other.*

He took a step, wavering slightly and resisting the urge to look down.

One step, two steps — almost there . . .

BZZZZZZZZZZZZZZ!

Suddenly the air was filled with a loud, violent hiss that seemed to come from everywhere at once. Startled, Tahu slipped, one foot sliding out over the nothingness. Just in time, he flung himself sideways, arms outstretched, regaining his shaky balance on the narrow beam.

Dozens of bright red creatures had appeared out of nowhere, swarming across the narrow bridge from both directions. Each was the size of a clenched fist and looked like a cross between a scorpion and a giant wingless firefly. Their deadly-looking pincers clamped open and shut rhythmically as they buzzed toward Tahu, their legs moving too fast to see.

"Hey!" Tahu cried in annoyance, kicking at several of the creatures that were already swarming up over his feet. "Get away!"

The glowing scorpions paid no attention. More and more of them swarmed around him, until they completely covered his legs.

"Ow!" he cried as one of them sank its pincers into his ankle. He smacked at it, but already two more of the creatures were clamping onto his knee and thigh.

"Enough of you," he muttered, pointing the sword just above the thickest cluster of the creatures on the bridge nearby. Focusing his energy, he blasted a spurt of flame, hoping to scare them away.

But the creatures merely glowed brighter, seeming to suck in the heat of the fire.

"What?" Tahu exclaimed. "So you like fire, eh, you stupid little pests? I'll show you fire!" He pointed his sword again, sending flame roaring out of the end of it. But once again, it only seemed to make the creatures stronger. The bridge, however, was glowing ominously as the stone started to melt beneath the intense heat.

"Uh-oh," Tahu said with a gulp as lava dripped off into the abyss.

The creatures were swarming thicker now, dozens of them clamping onto every part of his body.

Must . . . get . . . away. . . . Tahu thought desperately as he tried to shake them off.

How could he fight the scorpions? His best weapon — fire — seemed to be completely useless against them. And he was trapped on this bridge, forced to fight gravity and wind as well as the swarms of creatures.

Suddenly Gali's voice floated into his head: *Our best weapon is our minds.* That was what she had said back in the clearing. At the time, Tahu had paid little attention to her words. Now, though, they burned within his mind. And with them, suddenly, came an idea.

"Okay, pests," he said aloud. "Last chance to back off before it's too late. No takers? Oh, well, don't say I didn't warn you. . . ."

With that, he dropped his sword onto the bridge, then bent and grasped the stone with both hands. Flinging his feet off the edge, he let himself hang loose once again over the abyss.

He closed his eyes, picturing Lewa. The Toa of Air seemed unable to stand still for more than a few seconds and had spent much of the time back at the clearing doing backflips and handstands. At one point, Tahu remembered, Lewa had even jumped up and grabbed onto an overhanging branch and swung himself around it by both hands, flipping around and around.

Keeping that image in mind, Tahu swung his legs as vigorously as he could. It took a few tries, but finally he flung himself over the bridge and back around the other side. Gripping tightly with both hands, he pumped with his body, taking advantage of the momentum. He flipped around the narrow bridge again and again, building up speed.

Tahu spun faster and faster, and before long, the scorpion creatures started losing their grip. One by one at first, then dozen by dozen, they flew away into the darkness.

It's working! he thought gleefully. *It's working! They can't hold on!*

Still he kept spinning, around and around, until he felt the last fiery wounds of the creatures' pinches fade away and could no longer hear their buzzing. Only then did he slow down enough to flip himself back upright onto the bridge.

There, he thought, breathing hard from the effort. *Even Lewa would be impressed by that.*

He glanced up and down the bridge. There was no sign of the swarm in either direction. Then he felt a pinch and looked down to see that one scorpion creature had managed to hang on.

"I think I can handle one of you," Tahu said, yanking the creature loose. "Time to go join your — wait a second. What's that?"

He paused in the act of tossing the glowing creature into the chasm. What was on its head? Looking closer, he saw that it was wearing a tiny mask over its face. The mask was pitted and pockmarked. But it was a mask nonetheless.

"Strange," he muttered, poking curiously at the mask with his finger.

The small creature buzzed angrily, struggling against Tahu's grip. When his finger came close enough, it flung its pincers out and grabbed it, clamping down viciously.

"Ow!" Tahu yanked his hand away, once again winding up to throw the little beast down and be done with it. But again, something made him hesitate. Why would a creature such as this wear a mask?

He shifted his grip on the scorpion creature until he managed to trap its pincers within his hand. Then he used the other hand to carefully peel the little mask free.

As soon as he did so, the creature went limp in his hand. For a second he thought he'd accidentally killed it. But then its legs waved weakly, and it chittered woozily up at him.

He set the creature down on the bridge at his feet, being careful not to put his fingers within reach of its pincers. But he needn't have bothered with such caution. Showing no interest in him whatsoever, the little scorpion scurried quickly away down the bridge, disappearing a moment later into the darkness.

Tahu blinked, wondering what that might mean. Had the creature run away because he'd removed its mask? Or because it had suddenly realized it was now all alone in its attack?

He opened his hand, staring at the tiny mask. A gust of wind swooped past, nearly sending him off balance once again. It also swept the small mask off Tahu's palm and away into the chasm.

Tahu grabbed for it — but it was too late. The mask was gone. Blowing out a sigh of frustration, he did his best to shrug off the loss. The important thing was that he'd defeated the scorpion creatures. Now he could continue with his quest.

He picked up his sword. After all that had happened, the walk across the bridge no longer seemed quite so daunting, and it wasn't long before he was stepping onto the ledge.

The mask was lying there waiting, its empty eyeholes staring up at him blankly. He picked it up and settled it on over his own mask.

Energy exploded within him. He staggered forward, remembering the dropoff just in time to stop himself from stepping right over the edge.

So much power! He looked around, seeing his surroundings with new eyes aided by the mask's powers of X-ray vision. Even in the near darkness he could see the veins of minerals buried within the stone walls around him, the trickles of water cutting through the solid rock beneath his feet.

Tahu blinked, trying to get used to his new way of seeing. "Okay," he whispered to himself in awe. "Now we're getting somewhere. . . ."

COOL AS ICE

With every step, Kopaka cursed the heat, smoke, and choking ash of Ta-Wahi. Why did a Mask of Strength have to be hidden in such a place? He had no idea, and he hoped that the Matoran who had given him the tip had not led him astray.

Pausing as another wave of heat overwhelmed him, Kopaka raised his ice blade to his neck, letting its welcome coldness revive him. How could anyone spend any time on this infernal volcano, let alone live there?

An image of Tahu floated through his mind, and he grimaced. If the Toa of Fire could see him now, he would probably laugh his mask off.

Of course, I'd like to see Tahu trying to get along in Ko-Wahi, Kopaka thought. *He'd probably* melt a hole in a glacier and spend so much energy yelling at the ice that he couldn't climb out.

The thought amused him, giving him the strength to get moving again.

After a few more minutes of climbing, he crested a peak and found himself overlooking an amazing landscape. He knew it had to be what he was looking for: the Lava Lagoon.

Several of the slopes of the mountain met here, forming a deep, broad basin filled with lava. At least two hundred lengths across, the simmering lagoon glowed yellow and red and orange. A waterfall of lava poured into the far end, sending up constant sprays of steam and smoke.

Kopaka looked around, wondering where in this bubbling wasteland a mask might be hidden.

Then he noticed a small, craggy island jutting out of the center of the lagoon. Was the heat making him see things, or was that the gray shape of a Kanohi mask sitting on the island?

He groaned. Why couldn't the mask have been guarded by another Rahi instead — or two, or twelve? He would rather face all the Rahi on Mata Nui at once than have to deal with this.

Makuta showed quite a sense of humor when he hid these masks, he thought grimly. *But I'll have the last laugh — no matter what it takes.*

Pointing his ice blade at the lagoon, Kopaka focused his energy.

ZZZZZZZ*T!*

A small patch of lava froze — for about half a second. Then the ice cracked, steam escaped, and a moment later the frozen section had melted back into its original fiery form.

Kopaka frowned and tried again. But his efforts had little effect

Time for a new plan, he thought. *If I can't go straight across, maybe I can go over.*

Changing his focus, he concentrated on the steam in the air over the lagoon. He aimed his ice blade toward it.

ZZZZZZZ*T!*

The particles of moisture in the air froze solid, forming together into an icy bridge reaching over the first section of the lagoon.

ZZZZZZT!
ZZZZZZT!

Kopaka felt his energy draining away as he pointed his blade again and again. But when he was finished, he smiled with triumph. His ice bridge stretched all the way across the lagoon to the island!

Now all I have to do is go get that mask, he thought, stepping onto the near end of the bridge. He hurried forward a few steps, then paused. What was that sound?

Drip . . . SZZZZZ! . . . drip . . . SZZZZZ! . . . drip . . . SZZZZZ!

Glancing down, he saw with alarm that the bridge was already melting away.

"No!" he cried, pointing his blade toward it to refreeze it.

But it was no use. As fast as he could refreeze one section, another melted. Within seconds the middle part of the bridge collapsed into the lagoon. Kopaka barely had time to leap back to shore as his section of the bridge collapsed, too.

There had to be an answer. Turning the challenge over in his mind, Kopaka searched through his options.

Finally he had to admit the only likely solution: the other Toa. *If Tahu were here, he would have no trouble retrieving that mask,* Kopaka thought reluctantly.

He shook his head, annoyed with himself. Why waste thought on a solution that wouldn't work? He had found two masks already without help from the other Toa. He could find a way to get this one without them as well.

As he wandered toward the end of the little beach, Kopaka noticed a plume of steam coming from a crack in the rocky wall behind him. Unlike the sooty, smoky steam hovering over the lagoon itself, this steam looked pale and clean.

Curious, Kopaka climbed up the rocky wall for a look. He soon discovered a hot-water spring bubbling up from the depths of the mountain.

"Interesting . . ." he muttered.

He glanced out toward the island where

the mask lay, measuring the distance with his eyes. Then he stared again into the steaming spring. An idea was forming in his head.

He analyzed the information again and again. The depth and size of the spring. The distance to the island. The probable heat of the lava.

Still, he couldn't quite convince himself that it would work. The probability was fairly high, but nothing was certain. . . .

Kopaka clenched his fists as he imagined Tahu's mocking laughter, Lewa's perplexed glance. Neither of them would have the patience to waste so much time worrying over probabilities. Perhaps just this once he should live by their example.

Besides, it's this or nothing, Kopaka reminded himself. Of that, he was one hundred percent certain.

Not giving himself time to doubt his decision, Kopaka pointed his blade.

ZZZZZZZT!

The spring froze solid.

Kopaka smiled. As he had suspected, the water in the spring had been much cooler than the lava.

Now came the hard part — getting the miniature iceberg out of its hollow and down the slope to the lagoon. Little by little, Kopaka froze and then chipped away the outer wall of the hollow, until all he had to do was push the large chunk of ice straight out and over the edge.

There was no time to waste — the lava was already eating away at the edges of the ice floe. Without hesitating, Kopaka leaped down onto the ice.

Using the blade as a paddle, he rowed toward the island with all his might. The ice continued to melt, but Kopaka kept his gaze focused on his goal.

By the time he reached the rocky little ledge, his ice "boat" had melted away to about half its original size.

More than half, Kopaka told himself as he leaped onto the island and scooped up the mask.

*It's still more than half there. That will be enough —
especially with the added strength of my new Kanohi
to help me row.* He jammed the Mask of Strength
over his face, feeling its power seep through him.

Still, he hesitated as he stepped back onto
the floe. It would take him almost as long to row
back to shore as it had taken to get here. Would
the ice last that long?

Just go! he chided himself. *There's no other
choice.*

Jabbing his blade into the lava, Kopaka put
all the strength of his new mask into his effort as
he pushed away from the island.

I'll make it, he told himself firmly, squashing
the thought. *Whatever it takes, I'll do it. If the floe
melts away too soon, maybe I can freeze enough of
the lava to hop across the rest of the way a step at a
time. Or —*

As he jabbed his blade into the lava again,
he misjudged and hit the edge of the floe instead.
The force of the blow sent several large chunks
of ice flying — one straight toward him! The Ice

Toa didn't have time to dodge it. The ice chunk connected solidly with the side of his head, knocking him to his knees.

He clung woozily to the ice, fighting to retain consciousness. But darkness seeped out from the corners of his mind . . . and then, suddenly, an intense vision overwhelmed him, sweeping away the floe, the lagoon, the heat, and everything else.

First he found himself looking with a bird's-eye view over all of Mata Nui. The image suddenly rushed closer, almost as if he were falling straight toward the slopes of Mount Ihu in the center of the island. The image shifted slightly to one side, swooping down one of the mountain's slopes until it reached a large clearing. There, Kopaka saw a great temple built out of stone.

Then a strange, echoing voice spoke out of the darkness. *"Welcome, Toa of Ice,"* it said, fading in and out as Kopaka struggled to free himself from the vision. *"Do not be . . . your mind can journey to . . . behold the future of . . . you and the others shall . . . all the Great Masks of Power . . .*

together and defeat . . . three shall become . . . path
of wisdom . . . myself, Akamai . . . of the warrior . . .
only by uniting . . . farewell . . ."

With that, Kopaka's mind snapped back to
reality. He found himself on his hands and knees
on the floe, still clutching at the rapidly shrinking
chunk of ice.

*That little accident was bad luck on top of bad
judgment,* he thought bleakly as he finally faced
the truth — the ice floe wasn't going to make it
back to shore. That meant he had two choices:
Try the frozen-footstep method, or wait as long
as he could and then attempt an enormous leap
to solid ground.

He decided that the second plan had a
more likely chance of success. But the distance to
shore seemed impossibly far. . . .

Kopaka reminded himself that he now wore
the Great Mask of Strength. Perhaps it would give
his legs the extra power they would need to pro-
pel him such a tremendous distance. Perhaps . . .

Gathering his strength, Kopaka got into position and then waited. One long moment, then

another, then another, coolly patient as he gauged the footing beneath him. All he needed was enough to push off from —

"Now!" he shouted, leaping forward with all his might. The energy of the Pakari flowed through him, giving him extra strength.

But it wouldn't be enough.

That Great Mask of Levitation would come in awfully handy right now, he thought bleakly as he felt himself start to fall toward the bubbling lava.

"Kopaka!" a voice shouted from the direction of the shore.

Kopaka glanced forward, but saw only a flash of green as he suddenly felt himself caught up in a blast of wind.

"Aaaaaaah!" he cried as he flew helplessly through the air.

CRASH!

He smashed into the ground face first.

"Sorryoops, brother," Lewa's voice said from somewhere nearby. "I didn't have thought-time to plan a softer landing."

"Ugh," Kopaka groaned. Every limb in his

body ached. But he was still in one piece — and unmelted! "It's all right, brother Lewa," he added, realizing that it was Lewa's wind gust that had saved him. "I owe you one. I shall not forget this."

"Anytime, brother," Lewa said. "And at least I see you got a mask out of it."

Kopaka nodded, touching the new Kanohi on his face. He wondered if he should tell the other Toa about his vision. What had it meant? Who had sent it? Was it a foreshadowing of something important — or merely a trick sent by Makuta?

Whatever it was, it nearly got me boiled, he reminded himself. *Isn't that the best evidence of all that it must have come from Makuta?*

Disturbed by the thought, he remained silent about his vision as Lewa chattered on about finding his own Great Mask of Strength in Onu-Wahi.

"Had to fight a nastyugly Rahi to get it, too," he said cheerfully. "But I suppose it was worth it — gave that quickbreeze I sent you some extra oomph."

Kopaka nodded. "These Rahi — they seem to stop at nothing to guard these masks."

"Oh, this fellow quickstopped as soon as I knocked off its own mask," Lewa said. "It panicfled into the depths of the tunnels everquick."

"Really? Hmm." Kopaka filed that away in his mind. It could be useful to him later.

That reminded him — he still had masks to find. "My thanks to you again, brother Lewa," he said with a formal little bow. "Now I must take my leave and continue my search."

"Oh! I almost mindlost why I came looking for you in the first place," Lewa cried. "I just luckymet Onua and Pohatu downmountain. Onua has called a meeting."

Kopaka frowned. "But I haven't found all my masks yet."

"None of us has." Lewa shrugged. "We're all learnfinding that this searchquest is trickier than we thought. That's why Onua wants to get together. I'm not one for groupworking, but I think he may be right. We need to compare notes, do some teamplanning."

Kopaka opened his mouth to protest again, but shut it before speaking a word. How much time might he have saved just now if he'd had Lewa along in the first place — or Tahu, or Onua?

He sighed. As much as he hated the idea of joining in on some big, happy, crowded Toa-fest, the facts were staring him in the face. The mission would be more successful if the Toa attacked it as a team.

"All right," Kopaka said at last. "Let's go."

THE TEMPLE

Gali was very glad that Onua's meeting had gone more smoothly than the last. It had ended in one unanimous decision: The Toa would work as a team.

Each of the Toa had encountered at least one Rahi during their travels, and Gali was no exception. After encountering another of the monstrous swimming Rahi she'd seen just after her awakening, she respected the creatures' power more than ever. She now knew that such beasts were known as Tarakava. The Turaga had told them that all the Rahi were native beasts of the island — controlled by Makuta to do his dark bidding.

Perhaps when we've found all the masks, we'll also find a way to set the Rahi free, Gali thought.

She only wished that the mission were going more smoothly. They had wasted too much time on petty disagreements. Lewa kept getting distracted and wandering away from the group. Tahu seemed determined to completely disable every Rahi they encountered. Kopaka periodically got fed up with the bickering and threatened to go off again on his own.

Through it all, Gali did her best to maintain the peace. She could tell that Onua was working toward the same goal in a quieter way and found her respect for the strong, reserved Toa of Earth growing more and more. Now, as they approached the shoreline just south of Po-Koro, she glanced toward him.

"Onua," she said. "If what the Ta-Matoran told us is accurate, we will need to go beneath the waters to retrieve Tahu's levitation mask."

Lewa overheard her and groaned. "Not again!" he cried. "I already took one wetdive to get my Mask of Speed. I still haven't got all the wateryuck out of my ears!"

"Don't be foolish," Kopaka spoke up. "Obviously, only those among us who already hold the Kanohi Kaukau should go on from here. Pohatu, Lewa, Tahu — you can wait on the beach."

Tahu glared at him. "Thanks for pointing out the obvious," he retorted. "But it's my mask we're after here — my villager was the one who revealed its location. I think I should be the one to decide whether or not I go."

Gali rolled her eyes. "It would be helpful to have several of us standing guard on the beach, brother Tahu," she pointed out.

"That's true," Tahu admitted, though he still shot Kopaka an irritated glance. "Go with good fortune, Gali. We'll keep a careful watch for danger while we wait here for your return."

Onua was already leading the way into the surf, with Kopaka a step behind. Gali followed, feeling some of her anxiety wash away at the touch of the warm, familiar water. She dove into the waves, swimming quickly out into deeper water.

Soon the three of them reached the broad, open sweep of the sea valley.

Kopaka pointed to a large, shadowy shape visible in the water. Gali shuddered as she recognized the Tarakava.

"I escaped from one Tarakava by blinding it with waving seaweed, and from another by luring it into a cave where it got stuck," Gali told the others. "These Rahi are strong, but not very clever, I think. All we need is a plan. . . ."

Soon the three of them were swimming slowly toward the Tarakava. A moment later the creature spotted them and let out a roar.

"Okay, it knows we're here," Gali whispered, floating in place. "Kopaka, get ready."

The Ice Toa nodded. The Tarakava barreled toward them. Soon it was only a short distance away, then closer . . . Still Kopaka didn't move.

Gali held her breath. The beast would be upon them within seconds.

As she was about to cry out, the Ice Toa finally made his move. With a twitch of his ice blade, he sent a blast of intense cold out ahead of him, instantly freezing the water — and the Tarakava — into a solid block of ice.

"Nice work!" Onua cried, his deep voice rumbling through the water like an earthquake. "Now it's my turn. . . ."

With that, he struck the sandy ocean floor with his fists. The ground swelled up, arcing over the giant Tarakava ice cube until it completely surrounded the frozen area.

"That should hold it for a while," Gali said, relieved. "Now all we have to do is —"

"Wait," Onua interrupted, staring at the Tarakava, whose head protruded out of the dirt-and-ice mound that trapped it. "I just want to see something. . . ."

He swam toward the creature, carefully staying out of range of its jaws. Patting the dirt mound before him, he caused it to burst upward in a small explosion, knocking the Tarakava's mask from its face.

The creature's violent spasms stopped immediately. After a moment it let out a wail of dismay and started to wriggle again, but this time it completely ignored Onua.

"I thought that might happen," Onua said.

"When Pohatu and I encountered a pair of Nui-Rama, he knocked off the masks of one of them. The creature suddenly changed — flew away instead of continuing the fight."

Kopaka nodded thoughtfully. "Something similar happened when I met a Kuma-Nui on my way to Po-Wahi."

"I wish I'd mentioned it earlier," Onua said. "I didn't realize it might be important — until just now."

Gali noticed that Kopaka didn't make the same apology. "We have learned something important here, I think," she said. "It is through these masks that Makuta controls the Rahi." Noticing the gray shape of a mask against the white sand nearby, she darted forward to scoop it up.

"Mission accomplished," Onua said. "Come on, let's get back."

"Don't be stupid," Kopaka snapped. "You'll only end up killing yourself — and making a mess for the rest of us to clean up."

Pohatu sighed, wondering if it had been a

mistake to split into two groups. If Onua or Gali were here, maybe one of them could settle this argument between Kopaka and Lewa. But they, along with Tahu, had gone to Le-Wahi in search of Pohatu's second-to-last mask.

Now Pohatu stood atop the highest bluff in his own home region, staring at the mask that hung tantalizingly halfway down the sheer rock face. At the bottom of the cliff was an enormous Nui-Jaga. The Rahi knew the Toa were there — every few seconds, it turned its masked face toward them and rattled its tail stinger.

"Perhaps our icy brother is right, Lewa," Pohatu suggested. "If you miss your mark and fall — well, anyway, I'm sure we can find another way if we put our minds together."

Lewa shrugged, his smile never faltering. "Why worrybother?" he said. "After all, this way is so much more funnnnnnnnnn. . . ."

The last word was lost in a rush of movement as Lewa launched himself off of the cliff with both arms outstretched.

"That fool!" Kopaka muttered savagely.

Pohatu couldn't speak. He could only hold his breath, hardly daring to watch. It was his own Kanohi Kaukau that Lewa was trying to grab as he swept past — how could Pohatu live with himself if Lewa's bold attempt ended in catastrophe?

"Wheeeeeee!" Lewa cried, snatching the mask in one hand as he swooped past, then sweeping one arm through the air to call the wind to his aid. The sudden gust that resulted gave him a quick lift. But he soon left the wind behind, floating upward on his own power.

"He uses the Mask of Levitation well," Kopaka admitted grudgingly as he watched the grinning Lewa ascend toward them.

Pohatu shot a glance at the Ice Toa. Beneath all his coldness, Kopaka had an honest heart.

A second later Lewa landed beside them. "One Kanohi Kaukau, as ordered," he said breathlessly, tossing the mask to Pohatu. "Hope it fits, because I'd sorryhate to have to return it."

*　　*　　*

Onua squinted uncertainly toward the tree-tops. The sun was bright here in the rain forest of Le-Wahi, and his eyes ached with the effort of trying to see through its brightness.

"Is that it?" he asked Gali and Tahu, who stood beside him.

Gali nodded. "It is a Kanohi Kakama," she confirmed. "It seems to be stuck in the knot of this tree, up near the top. Too bad brother Lewa isn't here to play monkey for us."

"Indeed. Sister, you hold the Mask of Levitation — do you think you can get it?"

"I can try." Gali stared upward. "I haven't yet had much time to practice. But if I move slowly . . ."

Tahu let out a noisy, impatient sigh. "Look, we don't have all day for this," he said abruptly. "Why not try an easier way?"

With that, he pointed his sword at the tree.

"Tahu, no!" Gali cried.

But even as the words left her mouth,

flames shot out of Tahu's sword and enveloped the tree's trunk. Within seconds the fire had consumed the entire tree, burning it into a black skeleton sprouting from a pile of cinders. Only the mask remained untouched by the flame, falling intact to the ground with a puff of embers.

Onua frowned as he picked up the mask. *He'll set the whole forest ablaze!* he thought, as run-away flames licked at several neighboring trees.

Beside him, he saw Gali gesturing with her arms. A moment later, a drenching rain shower poured down over them, dousing all the fires.

"Thanks," Tahu said, wiping rainwater from his mask. "I didn't think the fire would spread."

"Right." Gali's voice sounded almost cold enough to have come from Kopaka. "I suppose you also didn't think about the birds who called that tree home, or the plants and animals that relied on it for shade. In other words, you didn't *think*."

With that, she turned and stalked off into the jungle.

* * *

"There!" Tahu crowed triumphantly as the de-masked Rahi scurried away down the drifts of lower Mount Ihu. "The Great Mask of Water Breathing is mine. And that means —"

"— all the masks have been found," Kopaka finished for him.

"Good," Gali said shortly, hardly smiling at Tahu's obvious glee as he placed the Kanohi Kaukau over his face and the dull gray surface of the mask suddenly gleamed bright red.

Kopaka was strangely pleased to notice that Gali and Tahu didn't seem to be getting along. He wondered what had happened between them, though he wasn't about to ask.

"Now we come to the next question," Onua said. "What are we supposed to do now?"

Tahu shrugged. "We have all our powers now," he pointed out. "So let's go take out the rest of the Rahi. Now that we know how to disable them —"

"Seems like timefoolery to me," Lewa interrupted. "The Matoran know the secret now, too. With that knowledge, they should be able to safekeep themselves against the Rahi for the nowtime. And I have a hunchthought that other tasks lay in store for us."

Kopaka winced at the Air Toa's comment. Didn't anyone else recognize how absurd it was to rely on hunches and premonitions? At the same time, though, he couldn't help flashing back to the vision he'd had on the Lava Lagoon.

Did it have some kind of meaning, or was he turning into a foolish dream-follower like Lewa himself?

"Perhaps our next duty has to do with the golden-colored Kanohi my Turaga mentioned," Gali said. "Does anyone know anything more about them?"

"Not I," Onua said as the others shook their heads. "What exactly were you told?"

"Not much." Gali frowned, looking puzzled and frustrated. "I — I suppose we will have to go back and ask. All I really know is that somehow, we are supposed to find such a golden mask."

Finally Kopaka spoke up. "I think I know where we might find it," he said quietly.

The others glanced at him in surprise. "Huh?" Tahu said. "What are you talking about?"

"I had a vision," Kopaka said. "Right before you found me on the Lava Lagoon, brother Lewa." He glanced at the Air Toa, who had stopped leaping around for once. "In it, I saw a temple — a huge temple at the center of the island. I think we're meant to go there."

Tahu snorted. "And when exactly were you going to let us in on this secret?"

"He just did, Tahu," Gali pointed out quietly. "And that's fine. There was no need of knowing it until now."

Kopaka gazed at her, touched that she'd come to his defense. *It's just because she's annoyed with Tahu over something or other,* he told himself.

Still, he couldn't help giving her a brief, grateful smile.

"It looks just as it did in my vision," Kopaka murmured, sounding surprised.

The others were already exclaiming over

the grand temple. But Onua's mind turned immediately to more practical matters.

"Look," he said, pointing to the life-size
carvings of the six Toa cut out of the temple walls,
complete except that the carvings wore no masks
at all. "Are you thinking what I'm thinking?"

"I am, if you're thinking our masks would fit
perfectly over these carved faces," Tahu said, rip-
ping off his Kanohi Kaukau and holding it over
the carved Tahu figure.

"Wait!" Kopaka said. "Let's not throw away
our powers foolishly."

Tahu frowned at him. "Who says we're
throwing them away?" he challenged him. "It was
your vision that led us here. Now you say we're
being foolish?"

"That's not what I meant," Kopaka said.

Gali placed a hand on Kopaka's arm. "It's
okay, brother," she said. "I think Tahu is on the
right track — this time."

"Thank you, sister Gali." Tahu smiled at her.
"I appreciate the support."

Gali smiled back, and Kopaka scowled in irritation. Whatever had been bothering those two earlier seemed to be over. Kopaka opened his mouth to argue further, but something stopped him.

Maybe this isn't the wrong thing to do just because it seems impulsive, he thought. Then he frowned. *What am I doing? Am I turning into Lewa or Gali, trusting passing whims and feelings?*

Tahu pushed his mask onto the stone Tahu's face. As the mask melted into the stone, he pulled off his Kanohi Miru, and then his other masks, placing each one onto the carving's face.

Lewa and Pohatu followed Tahu's lead. Even Gali stepped forward toward her sculpture, her Kanohi Akaku in hand.

Onua glanced over at Kopaka. "Normally I, like you, would be against this rush to move," he commented. "But I'm getting the strangest feeling that this is what we are meant to do."

Kopaka nodded. "I — I, too, am beginning to get that feeling."

That was enough for Onua. He had already observed enough to know that the Ice Toa wasn't one to make rash decisions — not without good reason, anyway.

The two of them walked over to their own likenesses. Onua pulled off his Kanohi Kakama. Taking a deep breath, he set it into place on the stone Toa's face. The stone seemed to suck it in, swallowing it into itself. Onua fed it another mask, and another. Soon he was placing his last mask onto the carving. It melted into the carving like the others but remained visible, tinting the stone black. Without any mask at all, Onua's face felt strange and vulnerable.

For a moment, nothing happened. Onua felt his heart sink. Had they just given away their Masks of Power for no good reason? Had this all been a trick of Makuta?

Then there was a peal of sound, like great bells blended with laughter. Onua gasped in amazement as a new mask suddenly appeared on the face of each stone carving — a golden Kanohi, glowing with light and power.

Onua carefully lifted the golden Kanohi from the carving's face and placed it on his own.

He staggered back a step as waves of power blasted through him. Then he smiled. This new mask united all the powers of the other six — only it was even stronger!

"So this was what we were really seeking," Gali said, sounding awed. "Now we truly have the power to take on the Makuta. . . ."

Her last few words were nearly drowned out by a mighty rumble from somewhere deep within the earth. The Toa jumped back as a group, even as the ground began to shake and groan beneath their feet.

A chasm yawned open in front of them, right in the middle of the main temple area. It turned into a tunnel about two lengths wide.

Then everything stopped. The earth lay still again, as if nothing had happened.

The Toa stared at the hole in the ground. Then they stared at one another. There was a moment of silence.

Finally Onua spoke.

"Come on," he said, stepping toward the tunnel. "I guess we'd better see where this goes."

INTO THE DARKNESS

Lewa's heart pounded with anticipation as the Toa made their way down the tunnel. But after so much confusion and uncertainty, it felt good to have a plan at last.

Follow tunnel, he thought. *Find Makuta. Destroy Makuta. Sounds plainsimple enough* . . .

The tunnel twisted and turned through the earth, traveling deeper and deeper. Tahu's sword cast enough of a glow to light their way, though deep, ominous shadows still lurked ahead.

Finally Tahu let out a shout as he turned a corner. "Hurry!" he cried. "I think we've found it."

"What?" Lewa skidded around the corner and stopped.

They were in a cavern, broad and long. Thick slashes of lightstone in the walls cast an eerie pale glow over the place. At the far end, an immense iron door filled most of the wall. Several other passageways snaked off in various directions along the sides of the cave, but Lewa didn't spare them a glance. His eyes were trained on that giant door.

"That's it," he whispered in awe. "That's where we'll find Makuta."

Nobody answered, but he could feel that they were all in agreement. Tahu gripped his sword tightly. "All right, then," he said. "If he's in there, let's go in and get him."

"Tahu, wait," Pohatu protested. "We can't just rush in there without a plan, or —"

SKREEEEEE!

A piercing shriek filled the room, echoing wildly. Whirling around, Lewa saw a pair of monstrous Rahi skittering out of two side passageways. They were immense, broad and squat but surprisingly fast. Their powerful arms ended in dangerous-looking pincers.

"What are those?" Pohatu cried.

Lewa gasped, recognizing the creatures from

a Turaga's description. "Manas. I rememberthink they're called Manas."

"They're just more Rahi," Tahu shouted, already swinging his fire sword. "Nothing we can't handle. Come on!"

Lewa hesitated — the Turaga had warned then that no single Toa could hope to take on the Manas. But perhaps together . . . He somersaulted through the air toward one of the creatures, landing on its back. He grabbed it and tried to flip it over, but it was larger than he'd expected and tossed him off easily.

"Oof!" he grunted, landing hard on the stone floor.

He leaped back into the fray, joining Tahu and Onua as they battled furiously against one of the Manas. Pohatu raced past, pausing long enough to whisper in Lewa's ear.

"Gali has set a trap," he said. "Help me lead the Manas toward that small tunnel back there."

Lewa nodded. Pohatu let out a whoop and raced to the back of the cave. Lewa jumped forward and smacked the nearby Manas on its shell-like back before somersaulting away. "Catch me if you can, uglypincher!" he taunted.

The Manas paused, turning toward him. But then it returned its attention to Onua, snapping at him with its deadly claws.

"This way, brother," Lewa shouted, waving his arms at Onua. "Run this way."

Onua managed to dodge the creature's blows and raced toward Lewa. "What is it, brother?" he asked breathlessly.

"A plan," Lewa told him. "Come on, we need to lead them this way."

Nearby, he saw that Kopaka was doing his best to lure the second Manas in the same direction. He wielded his ice blade coolly, backing up a few steps each time the Manas lunged at him. Beside him, Gali served as a distraction whenever the creature seemed to be getting the better of the Ice Toa.

Step by step, the six Toa led the Manas toward the tunnel. Lewa glanced behind him, noting the water lapping at the mouth of the tunnel.

He didn't know the details of the plan, but he could guess them.

If we can get this monsterpair trapped in that tunnel, sister Gali can ask the waters to awaycarry them, he thought. *Then we can stoneblock the tunnel, and get back to finding Makuta.*

Lewa felt his body quivering with eagerness to move, but he forced himself to wait. They had to act together, or the plan would fail.

When Gali spoke, it was a single word. "Now," she said.

The Toa all acted at once. Lewa, Tahu, Pohatu, and Onua rushed forward and leaped past or over the two Manas, putting the creatures between themselves and the tunnel. Meanwhile, Gali rushed closer to the tunnel's entrance, and the waters within started to churn.

But what is our icebrother doing? Lewa wondered even as he began to swing his blade at the Manas, driving them back.

He soon understood. As the water in the tunnel entrance splashed out onto the cavern floor, Kopaka pointed his ice blade at it, freezing it solid. Soon a slick coating of ice covered much of the floor between the Manas and the tunnel. Once the creatures reached the ice, it would be easier to push them into the watery trap.

"Almost there!" Tahu shouted. "Come on, brothers! Let's finish this!"

Lewa leaped forward again, swinging at the closer of the two Manas. The creature hissed furiously, striking back with deadly accuracy. Its claw struck the Air Toa on the shoulder, sending him rocketing backward.

Ignoring the pain in his shoulder, he leaped back into action. The Manas took another step backward, then another . . . until it finally hit the ice.

"Push!" Tahu howled, hurling himself at the creature. By this time Kopaka had joined the fighters, and the five of them leaped at the two Manas, shoving them toward Gali's tunnel.

Lewa could see the creatures' claws striking his comrades again and again — he felt powerful blows land on his own body. But he ignored the pain. All that mattered was the plan. . . .

The Manas skittered across the ice, heading straight toward the tunnel.

"Come on!" Tahu shouted, pointing his fire sword at the ground to melt the ice that now lay between the Toa and their quarry. "Don't give them a chance to escape."

But before the Toa could reach the Manas to give them a last push into the cave, the two crablike creatures spun toward each other. Hissing loudly, each of them reached out its claws, locking them together until they seemed to merge into one even more enormous creature.

"Oh, no!" Onua cried. "Look at them — they're too big for the tunnel now!"

"They're working together," Kopaka said grimly. "I didn't think the Rahi were capable of such intelligence."

Pohatu shook his head. "These Manas creatures are not ordinary Rahi."

Lewa was already leaping into action. "We

are not planlost yet," he cried. "I'll separate them if I can. . . ."

Without waiting for a reply, Lewa somersaulted forward. He crashed headlong into the tangle of claws that held the two Manas together.

The creatures let out a furious hiss. Acting together, they swung their joined claws outward, sending Lewa flying across the cave. He smashed against the wall and landed in a heap, dazed.

As he climbed to his feet, he saw the paired Manas bounce off of the too-small tunnel entrance. Soon they had rocketed back across the remains of the ice onto dry ground. There, they separated and returned their attention to the surprised Toa.

These are no ordinary Rahi, Lewa thought as he saw the Manas' pincer land a powerful blow on Tahu, knocking him into the wall. *No ordinary Rahi at all.*

THE POWER OF SIX

Kopaka saw Tahu fly by and crash into the wall. As the Fire Toa slid to the floor, stunned, Kopaka aimed his ice blade in front of the Manas that was moving in on the fallen Toa. The floor in front of the creature instantly froze once again, slowing it down long enough for Lewa to somersault in and drag Tahu out of range.

"This is ridiculous," Gali cried as she defended herself against the second Manas. "They're just too strong! We'd better retreat."

"Never!" Tahu croaked, his voice hoarse but determined. "We must stay united. We must defeat them!"

Kopaka blinked, wondering why Tahu's words had struck such a chord in his mind. *Where have I heard something like that before?*

He glanced toward Gali and found her watching him. "What is it, brother?" she asked. "Do you know something? I — I think I do. I had a vision. It told me that something would happen after we found all the Masks of Power. That we would need to — unite."

Kopaka hesitated. Could it be?

The words from his vision returned: . . . *behold the future . . . you and the others shall . . . all the Great Masks of Power . . . together and defeat . . . three shall become . . . path of wisdom . . . myself, Akamai . . . of the warrior . . . only by uniting . . .*

"I think I had the same vision," he admitted at last. "I didn't understand it at the time. I — I still don't understand it."

"Don't you see?" Gali stared into his eyes, almost seeming to forget about the Manas, who were attacking the other Toa nearby. "I was told that three shall become Wairuha and walk the path of wisdom. Three shall become Akamai and walk the path of the warrior. Only by uniting will the Toa find the strength to triumph."

Kopaka shook his head. "No," he said. "It

doesn't make sense. How could such a thing happen?"

"I sense that it will happen if we want it to," Gali replied quietly. She glanced briefly toward the battle behind them. "I'm thinking that *I* want whatever will help us all. Do you?"

Kopaka stared at her for a moment. How could he want such a thing? Three become one — it would mean giving up his own individuality. No! It was impossible. . . .

Or was it? *Haven't I found that sometimes my own powers fell short?* he thought reluctantly. *Haven't I found myself wishing at times that the others were with me?*

Gali was still watching him. "Unity, duty, destiny," she said urgently. "Think about those words, brother. Do you believe in them?"

"Yes," Kopaka said at last. "Yes. I don't like them much right now, but I believe in them." He took a deep breath. "Let's do it."

"Brothers!" Gali shouted. "We need to retreat — just for a moment."

Pohatu and Onua glanced at each other.

Then they used their powers simultaneously to tumble down part of the ceiling and create a wall of rubble right in front of the advancing Manas.

"That won't hold them for long," Pohatu said breathlessly. "Now, what is it?"

Gali quickly described the vision she'd had. "We need to unite," she finished. "Combine our powers. Otherwise, there is no hope of victory."

The others nodded. "At this point," Tahu said, "I'll try anything."

As if part of one of his own dreams, Kopaka moved toward Gali and Lewa. Nearby, Tahu turned to face Pohatu and Onua. In each group, three Toa locked eyes . . . and became one.

THE TOA UNITE

The two Toa Kaita were a worthy match for the powerful Manas, and this time, the battle raged more furiously than ever.

Akamai fended off one with a series of powerful blows. "What, you scurry away like a tiny Hoto bug?" he cried with a roar of laughter.

"Do not taunt them, Akamai," Wairuha said. "Remember that they are unwilling servants of Makuta. Let us finish this quickly."

The words had hardly left his mouth when one of the Manas leaped at him. Despite his immense strength, the strike sent Wairuha staggering backward a few steps as the enemy clamped its pincers onto him. Using all of his strength, Wairuha managed to rip the Manas free and fling him against the wall.

The Manas hit the stone with a solid crunch. But it recovered quickly and skittered back toward the battle.

Turning toward the Manas that was scurrying toward him, Wairuha sucked in a deep breath, feeling his powers — of ice, water, and wind — expand and merge within him. A moment later, a raging blizzard erupted in the cavern.

Akamai, too, was using his combined powers. A giant crater exploded in the cavern floor, spraying stone, earth, and lava in every direction. Another crater appeared, and another, until the Manas were trapped on an island of solid floor surrounded by a moat of boiling lava.

Wairuha focused his energy through the blizzard, controlling it. He concentrated with everything he had — logic, instinct, and impulse guiding him all at once. Soon he had compressed the might of the storm into a single, focused beam of pure cold energy.

He turned it toward the trapped Manas. As the beam passed over them, the creatures froze solid.

"Nice work, brother," Akamai said. "But I fear it will take more than that to kill them."

Wairuha was already moving toward the lava moat. "There is no need to kill them, brother," he said. With one acrobatic leap, he crossed the moat and stood beside the frozen Manas. "I'll need your assistance to remove these masks."

Akamai nodded and leaped over as well. Touching one finger to the mask of one of the Manas, he soon melted the ice surrounding it. Wairuha reached out and pulled it free, dropping it into the lava, where it sank out of sight.

The Toa Kaita turned to the other Manas, repeating the process. Soon both Manas were free of their controlling masks.

"There," Wairuha said, leaping back across the moat. "That takes care of that."

"Not quite." Akamai bent and touched the ground at the edge of the lava moat. There was a rumble, as the edges moved toward each other, closing off the moat as if it had never existed.

Wairuha looked around. Except for the

frozen forms of the Manas, the cave looked as empty and peaceful as when the Toa had arrived.

"Our work is done," he said. "And now . . ."

He felt his mind slipping away, as if in the moment just before sleep. He closed his eyes. . . .

Tahu opened his eyes. *Is it really me?* he wondered.

Yes. He was himself again. Becoming part of Toa Kaita Akamai had been electrifying, but it was nice to have his own mind and will to himself again.

Glancing around, he saw the other Toa standing nearby, all of them looking as dazed as he himself felt.

Lewa was the first to speak. "Well," he said, stretching and bending. "That was a powerfeeling that you don't get every day."

Laughter bubbled from Gali like a spring. "Brothers," she cried, stretching her arms wide. "We did it! We became a part of something larger — and did what we never could have done otherwise."

OUT OF THE SHADOWS

"Quicklook!" Toa Lewa cried, pointing across the huge underground cavern. "The Manas are thawing. Once Makuta sees his hardluck creatures running for their lives, he'll be out of our way everquick."

Pohatu glanced where the Air Toa was pointing. He and the other five Toa watched as the mask-free Manas thawed from the deep freeze that Toa Kaita Wairuha's icy power had put them in and scuttled away, disappearing into the darkness of a nearby tunnel.

It had been a hard-fought victory for the Toa. A moment worthy of celebration. Somehow, though, Pohatu found it impossible to relax and enjoy it. There was something — a shudder of stone against stone, the faintest tremor in the rocky ground — that told him there might be more to come.

The Toa of Earth was thinking along much the same lines. "Don't be so certain that we have truly defeated the Great Evil One," Onua warned Lewa solemnly. "While these Manas were powerful, they were but guardians. Makuta himself —"

"What's that?" Gali interrupted. The Water Toa was staring intently toward the back of the cavern. "Something moved back there. Onua, can you see anything?"

Kopaka peered into the darkness along with the others, gripping his ice blade uneasily.

Drip. Drip.

Water trickled onto stone somewhere far off — or was it nearby? Down here it was hard to tell.

"Does anyone see anything?" Lewa's whisper broke the near silence.

"Shh!" Gali chided him. "Did you hear —"

CREEEAAAAAAAAAAK!

The sudden sound exploded through the cave.

"*Toa . . .*"

Pohatu spun around. Had he really just heard that whisper?

"*Toa . . .*"

"Who is it?" Tahu called boldly. "Who's there? Step forward and reveal yourself at once, or suffer the wrath of Toa Tahu!"

Mocking laughter echoed through the underground chamber. "But of course," a low, reverberating voice hissed with delight. It seemed to be coming from nowhere and everywhere at once. "Toa Tahu, with a heart of fire and a temper to match. Just how hot can you burn?"

Makuta. Without knowing how he knew, Tahu's mind formed the name.

This, then, was the Dark One they had sought for so long.

There was a glimmer of movement in one of the tunnels leading off from the larger central chamber. Tahu leaped toward it instantly and struck with all his strength. But his fire sword sliced through empty air.

"Wait!" Pohatu cried, even though it was

too late. "Tahu, wait a moment. We don't even know what it is we face yet."

Once again, laughter filled the chamber. "Ah, and this must be the famous Toa Pohatu, with a mind like a stone," the mysterious voice cooed. "Always ready to wait and watch and ponder — even as Mata Nui crumbles around him."

"It is easy enough to mock us from the shadows," Onua said evenly, stepping into the center of the chamber. "But your words will never defeat us."

"No doubt," the voice responded silkily. "But it matters not, as I have only to sit back and watch as you defeat yourselves."

Confused, Gali waited to hear more. But the voice had faded away, as if it had never been.

"What was that supposed to mean?" Lewa asked, breaking the silence.

Before Gali could answer, she caught a flash of movement out of the corner of her eye. Spinning to face it, she saw a dark figure racing toward Tahu, wielding a deadly-looking sword.

TOA VS TOA

"Tahu! Look out!"

The Fire Toa turned just in time to raise his sword against the onslaught. The face of his attacker was hidden behind a blackened, pitted mask, and black smoke billowed from its sword.

Tahu held the stranger off as best he could. He channeled the power of his flame through his fire sword, pointing it toward the sandy ground beneath his attacker. It instantly crystallized into glass and broke under the stranger's weight. The attacker plummeted out of sight.

But Tahu barely had time enough to smile before the stranger leaped out of the pit. "Hate to shatter your illusions," it said in a sizzling, crackling voice, "but it will take more than that to get rid of me."

The words only drove Tahu to greater fury. He shot white-hot flames out of the sword, but his movements were too fast, careless, striking the walls and boulders of the cavern until sparks flew in all directions, showering over the other Toa.

"Take care, Tahu," the attacker spoke again, "lest the fire of your anger blaze out of control."

Tahu gritted his teeth. "We'll see how you like my fire now," he said.

He pointed his sword at the stony cavern floor. Fire poured from the end, melting the rock into steaming, glowing lava.

"Brother Tahu!" Onua's voice sounded distant, almost lost in the bubbling sound of the boiling lava. "Watch what you're doing — you'll endanger us all!"

Tahu's mysterious opponent leaped off its rock and surfed across the bubbling lava. Its smile broadened. "Come, give in to the flame," it whispered. "Let it consume you and all you hold dear — I know you can feel it burning deep inside."

Tahu gasped, startled out of his own anger. What sort of enemy was this? He looked around for help and saw that five more attackers had suddenly appeared, as if out of the shadows themselves, each moving in on a different Toa. . . .

Nearby, Gali struggled against another mysterious attacker. The stranger's form mirrored her own, but rather than the clean blue of the open sea, its body was the muted, sickly brownish-black of an oil slick.

"Who are you?" Gali gasped as she released a raging flood of water toward her attacker.

A chuckle poured out of the attacker, who seemed unaffected by the flood. "Who am I?" it said. "Is the wise, all-seeing Gali really so blind? I am — *you!*"

Pohatu jumped atop an enormous boulder just in time to avoid being swept away by Gali's flood. "Hey!" he cried, his usual good nature overwhelmed by near panic. "Gali, take care not to fight your friends as well as your enemy!"

His opponent smirked. "So much for teamwork," it said in its gravelly voice. "This is how your friends repay your loyalty. Makes one wonder why one should bother with friends at all, doesn't it?"

"Not at all." Pohatu leaped to the ground and immediately swung his weapon at the boulder. It shattered into hundreds of flying shards, ricocheting off the walls toward the mysterious attacker.

The stranger laughed as he dodged the rocks. "Too bad, Pohatu," it taunted. "Good thing you expect nothing in return for your loyalty to your friends. Because now that the chips are down, it seems they've left you to fight me all alone."

It was getting hard for Lewa to concentrate on his own battle. First he'd nearly backflipped into the pool of lava that had suddenly appeared to cover half the cave. Then a flood of water had washed through.

"AI-AI-AI-AI-AI!" he yodeled, flipping himself up and over his attacker's weapons and out of the boulder's path.

CRRRRAAAAAACK!

The cavern shuddered as the boulder struck the wall. Lewa glanced hopefully back toward it, wondering if his opponent might be trapped behind it.

"Looking for me, Toa of Air?"

What is this creature, this quickdodging darkstranger? Lewa wondered as he leaped into the air to escape another blow. *It looks like me — but not like me.*

He took in the stranger's pitted mask, blackened as if by a creeping forest mold. Its skin beneath was green — the washed-out green of a diseased leaf.

Tumbling out of range and lifting his arms, Lewa focused his energies on the air all around him. Soon a whirlwind roared through the cavern. It swept up Lewa's enemy, and the Toa of Air laughed with delight.

But his opponent merely laughed in return as it glided easily through the currents and soon landed back beside the startled Toa.

*   *   *

It hadn't taken Kopaka long to realize what was happening — Makuta had created these shadowy versions of the Toa to challenge them where the Manas and all his other creatures had failed.

And so far, the plan seemed to be working.

Kopaka fought on grimly. Neither he nor his enemy was wasting any energy on words. Kopaka found his frustration rising as each of his carefully executed moves was met and returned with equal precision.

This isn't working, he thought. *There has to be a better way.* . . .

"This should cool you off," he muttered.

He touched his ice sword to the ground and focused his energy. Instantaneously, the cavern floor froze into a solid sheet of ice.

Even as he did it, Kopaka realized he'd miscalculated. His enemy smiled as it glided across the ice, its moves more graceful and controlled than ever.

"I see you've just recognized the cold, hard truth," it whispered in a voice as sharp as an icicle.

*　　*　　*

Onua shook his head, willing himself to focus, to think through this problem. He had already tried overpowering his enemy with raw strength, but its might matched his own. He had attempted to trap it by tunneling through the cavern wall and then collapsing the tunnel atop it, but the creature had burrowed out easily.

We can't go on this way, he thought desperately.

Right now the Toa were at an impasse, evenly matched with their enemy. But if even one of them went down, it could mean the end of all of them.

Feeling uncharacteristically desperate, the Earth Toa struck the ground before him with all his might. The earth rumbled at the blow, shaking the entire cavern and sending a hailstorm of rocks and earth raining down on all the fighters.

Onua felt despair grip him as he saw that while the other Toa had been knocked off their feet, his own opponent merely leaped over the torn earth and moved in to press the attack.

UNITY, DUTY, DESTINY

Kopaka hit the ground hard as the quake rumbled beneath him. His enemy was on him in a flash.

He managed to block the blow with his shield and then swing his ice blade upward. If he could just aim . . .

SKREEEEEEEK!

Kopaka smiled as he saw that his enemy was frozen in place. Kopaka sent the frozen enemy skittering across the ice until it smashed into the cavern wall. The creature shattered into hundreds of icy shards.

And each of the ice shards was forming into a new enemy!

Nearby, Onua glanced over and gasped when he saw Kopaka's predicament.

This is bad, Onua thought helplessly, dodging another blow from his own enemy. *How can I fight one so much like myself? How can any of us?*

He blinked as the answer dawned on him at last. Of course!

"Listen up!" he shouted. "We're going about this all wrong. We can't hope to defeat our own shadow doubles — but that's why we're a team!" He wanted to say more, but he didn't have the chance — he had to dive aside to avoid another blow from his opponent's weapon.

Pohatu heard Onua's words, but he couldn't respond for a moment. He was too busy fending off his own attacker. But in the back of his mind, he turned over the Earth Toa's plan and found that it made sense.

"Who are you kidding?" his opponent chortled mirthlessly, as if reading his thoughts. "They're not going to fight *for* you, Toa of Stone, or even *with* you. They'll use your strength to save themselves, then leave you behind."

"No," Pohatu said firmly, putting all his strength into one leg as he shattered another boulder with a mighty kick. His enemy fell back to avoid the shrapnel of stone, but instead of pressing the advantage, Pohatu spun away and glanced quickly around the cavern.

He saw the Fire Toa desperately trying to fend off a volley of blows with his fire sword. "Tahu!" Pohatu shouted. "Stand back!"

Gathering his energy, he leaped upward and struck the ceiling of the cave with a mighty blow of his fist. As the pieces broke off and fell, Pohatu directed them straight onto the Fire Toa's opponent.

"Aaaaaaaah!" the smoky stranger cried, raising its arms to protect itself. Flames shot out of its sword, but it was no use. It couldn't melt the falling stones fast enough. Within seconds it was buried beneath a mound of rocky debris.

Tahu stared at Pohatu in surprise. "What did you do that for? I was just about to —"

"Never mind," Pohatu yelped, turning to defend himself against his opponent. "Help Gali!"

Tahu glanced over his shoulder and saw that

the Water Toa was on the ground at the edge of the lava pool, her enemy advancing upon her.

"Gali!" Tahu cried. "Hold on, I'm coming!"

"Tahu!" Gali gasped. "Don't — this thing is too strong!"

But Tahu didn't hesitate. As the Shadow Gali whirled to face him, he pointed his fire sword. Heat and flame danced out from the end, wrapping around the enemy as it howled in surprise.

Steam hissed out in all directions, obscuring his view. When it faded, nothing remained of the Shadow Gali but a puddle on the cavern floor.

The defeat of two of the shadow enemies gave the other Toa new strength of purpose. Gali re-formed her flood and sent it gurgling toward the Shadow Onua. It cried out in dismay as water pounded against it, eroding it away into nothing but a bit of sand.

The distraction gave Onua the chance to help Lewa. Seeing that the Air Toa's enemy was somersaulting high in the air out of reach, Onua quickly summoned the earth beneath his feet to rise up, trapping the high-flying enemy in a floor-to-ceiling column of dirt and stone.

Freed from his enemy, Lewa saw that Kopaka and Pohatu alone remained under attack.

While Pohatu was holding his own, the ice-shard enemies had Kopaka surrounded.

"I'm coming!" Lewa shouted, tumbling through the air around the icy battle. "Kopaka!" he cried. "DUCK!"

The Ice Toa looked startled, but threw himself to the floor. A split second later, the whirlwind roared down around him, grabbing the shard soldiers into its grasp and spinning them around and around at dizzying speed.

The icy shard-soldiers crashed against one another again and again. Before long they had disintegrated into tiny sparkles of ice.

"Bad move," Kopaka said bleakly. "What if they all form into enemies again?"

"Not a problem," Tahu said, blasting the ice

crystals with his fire sword. Within seconds, they had melted and evaporated into steam.

"Guys?" Pohatu called breathlessly. "Um, hey — anyone want to give me a hand here?"

The Toa of Stone was still trading blows with his shadow self. "Oops!" Lewa said.

"I'll take care of this," Kopaka said. "Stand back."

Taking a deep breath, the Ice Toa blew out a frosty blast, freezing the area around Pohatu into a sheet of ice. The Shadow Pohatu skidded across, winding up in Tahu's pool of lava, where it sank with a gurgle.

Drip. Drip. Drip.

Once again, the cave was nearly silent. The Toa stood there for a long moment, staring at one another. Then, as a group, they collapsed wearily to the ground.

After catching his breath, Tahu sat up and glanced at Onua, who was watching the others thoughtfully. "What do you think, brother?" he asked the Earth Toa.

Onua smiled, though there was a hint of wariness in his eyes. "I think," he said, "that we have won an important battle, and of that we can be proud. But there is more to come."

Tahu nodded, his grin fading as he gripped his fire sword more tightly. Yes, Onua was right. He could feel it, burning in his mind like a half-remembered dream.

There was much more to come.